For Tom and Daisy

Text copyright © 1993 by Jill Leman

Illustrations copyright © 1993 by Martin Leman

First published in Great Britain by Orchard Books

Printed in Belgium

Library of Congress Cataloging in Publication Data

Leman, Jill. Sleepy kittens/by Jill Leman; illustrations by Martin Leman.—

1st U.S. ed. p. cm. Summary: Sleepy kittens can be found in many places around the house, but never in their

special box. [1. Cats—Fiction. 2. Sleep—Fiction. 3. Stories in rhyme.] I. Leman, Martin, ill. II. Title. PZ8.3.L53955SI

1994 [E]—dc20 93-24232 CIP AC ISBN 0-688-13288-X (trade). — ISBN 0-688-13289-8 (lib.)

First U.S. edition, 1994

1 3 5 7 9 10 8 6 4 2

SLEEPY KITTENS

JILL AND MARTIN LEMAN

TAMBOURINE BOOKS  NEW YORK

Three kittens feel like napping.
Where? Where? Where?

Up on the table,

Or down on the chair.

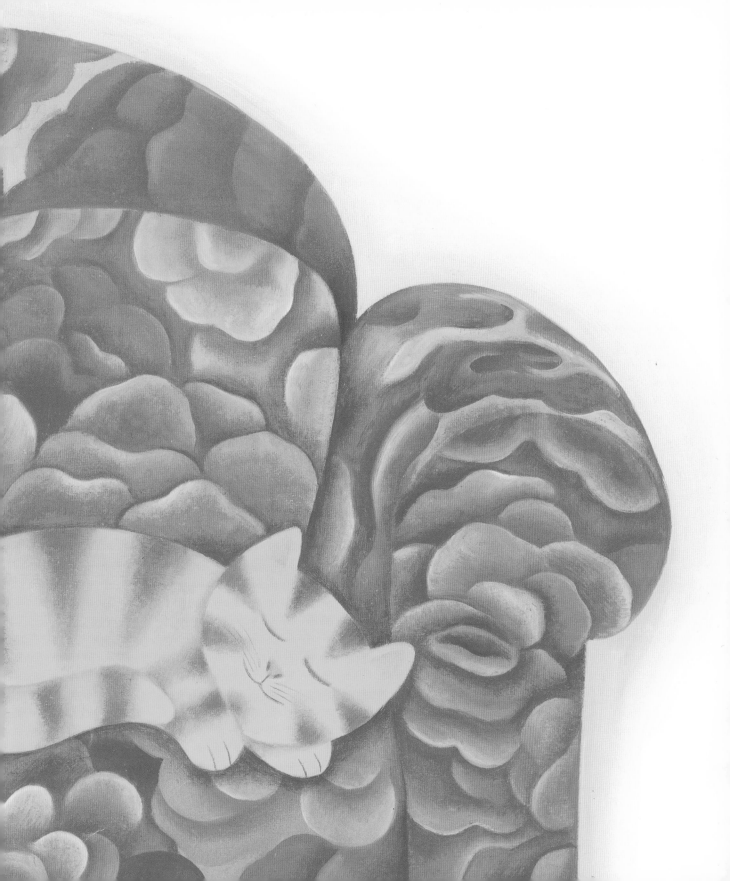

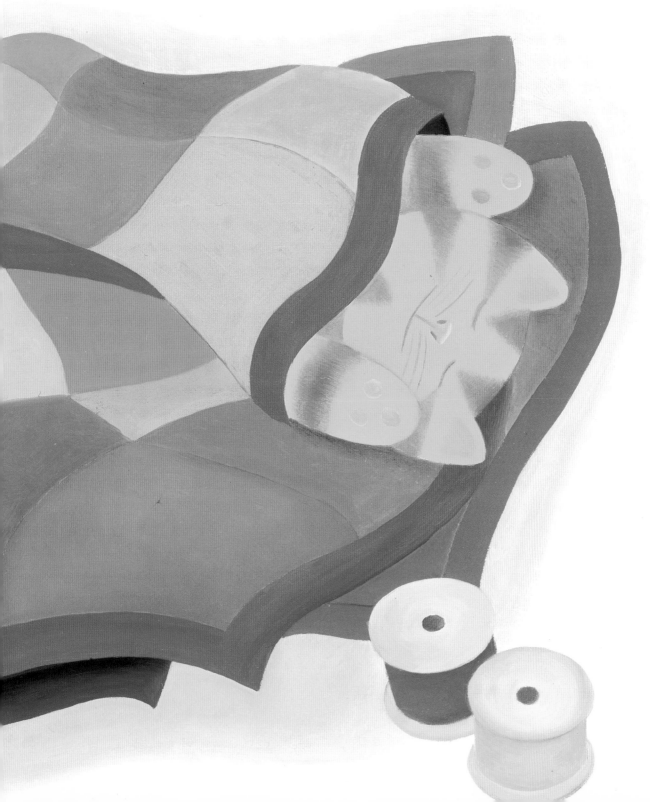

Under Mommy's sewing,

All over Granny's hat,

Snuggling next to Fido,

Or across a cuddly lap.

In front of a warm hearth,

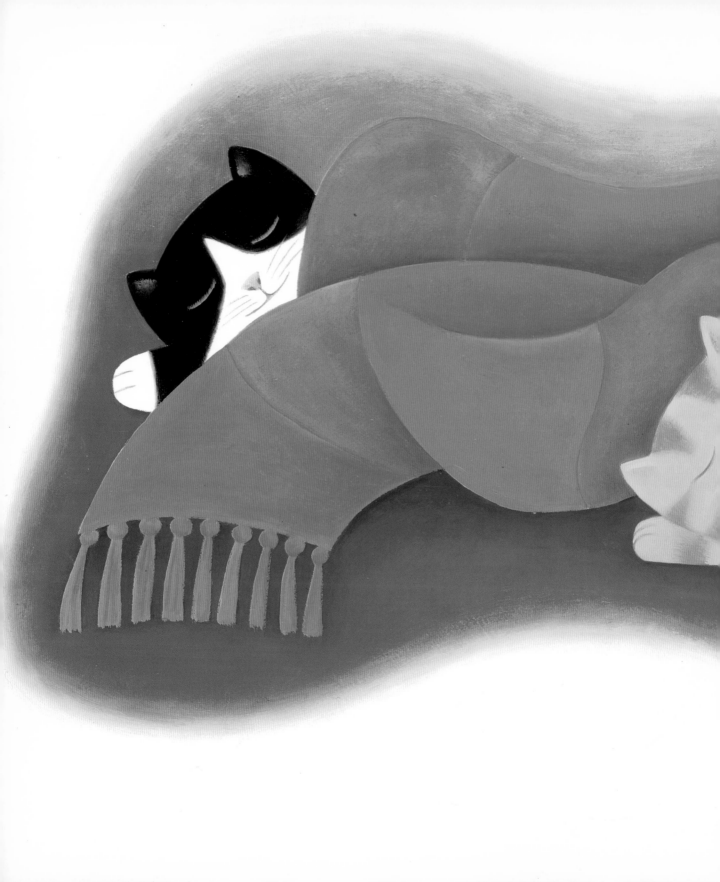

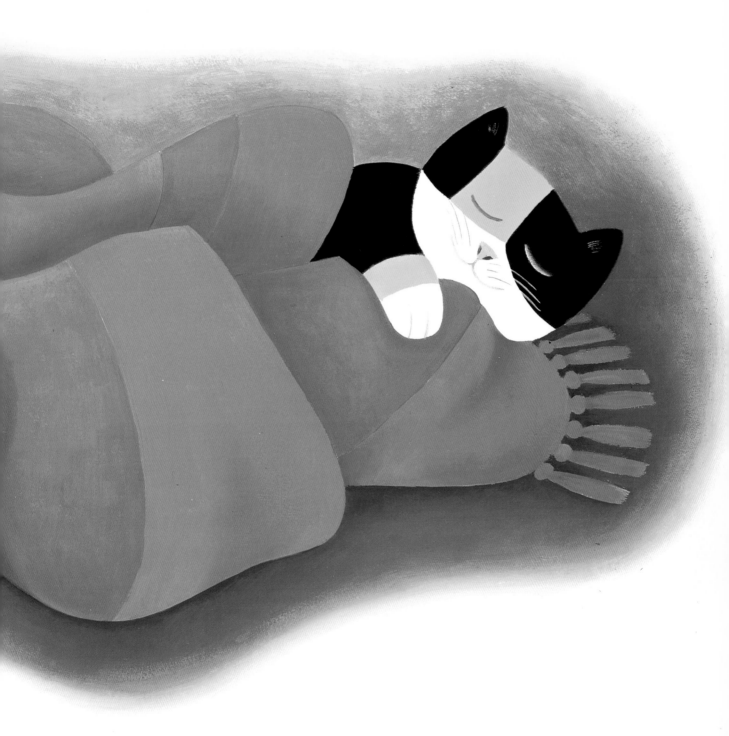

Or behind a woolly scarf,

Or in a drawer
between the socks,

But never in their special box!

They're always where they shouldn't be,

Even in my bed with me. Good night!